Shep the Sheep of Caladeen

Written by
Laura Appleton-Smith

Illustrated by
Carol Vredenburgh

Curriculum

Laura Appleton-Smith holds a degree in English from Middlebury College.
Laura is a primary school teacher who has combined her talents in creative writing with
her experience in early childhood education to create *Books to Remember*.
She lives in New Hampshire with her husband, Terry.

Carol Vredenburgh graduated Summa Cum Laude from Syracuse University and has worked
as an artist and illustrator ever since. Now happily settled in New Hampshire, Carol thoroughly enjoyed
the adventure of illustrating this book and getting to know Shep.

A Book to Remember™
Published by Flyleaf Publishing

For orders or information, contact us at **(800) 449-7006**.
Please visit our website at **www.flyleafpublishing.com**

Fifth Edition 12/11
Library of Congress Catalog Card Number: 99-90770
ISBN-13: 978-1-929262-02-1
Printed and bound in the USA at Worzalla Publishing, Stevens Point, WI. 12/11

Chapter 1

The king and queen of Caladeen lived in a castle on top of a hill.

All around the castle was a big green field, and down the steep hill was the deep green sea.

In the field around the castle lived the queen and king's royal sheep.

The sheep were free to eat the royal grass, drink from the royal stream, and sleep on leaf beds under the royal trees.

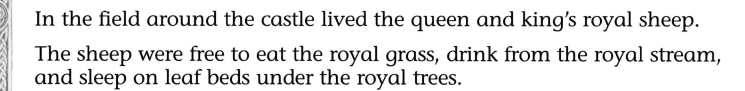

4

Each royal sheep had a different name,
and a ribbon of a different color around its neck.

On each ribbon hung a bell with a different ring
so the king and queen could hear the sheep
even if they could not see them.

In the evenings, the king and queen would visit the royal sheep.

They would pat them and feed them from big baskets of royal carrots.

At night, the queen and king
fell asleep to the ringing bells
on their sheep's necks.

You see, the king and queen
of Caladeen had never
had children, so their sheep
were very dear to them.

Chapter 2

The queen and king had a team of royal sheep keepers.

Their job was to keep the sheep clean and trim their fleece when it got long.

Baskets of cut fleece went to royal spinners, weavers, and seamstresses.

Their job was to make the queen beautiful dresses and the king beautiful jackets from the sheep's fleece.

The royal sheep were pleased to see the king and queen
dressed in fabric from their fleece. It made them feel important.

But Shep was different. His fleece was long and had never
been trimmed to make a beautiful dress or jacket.
This made Shep feel sad and unneeded.

Chapter 3

If the queen and king did not need him, Shep felt he must leave. Shep had a plan...

He would sneak from the royal field. He would leap the royal wall and run to the sea. He would see a ship that could take him from Caladeen. His plan was to leave the next night.

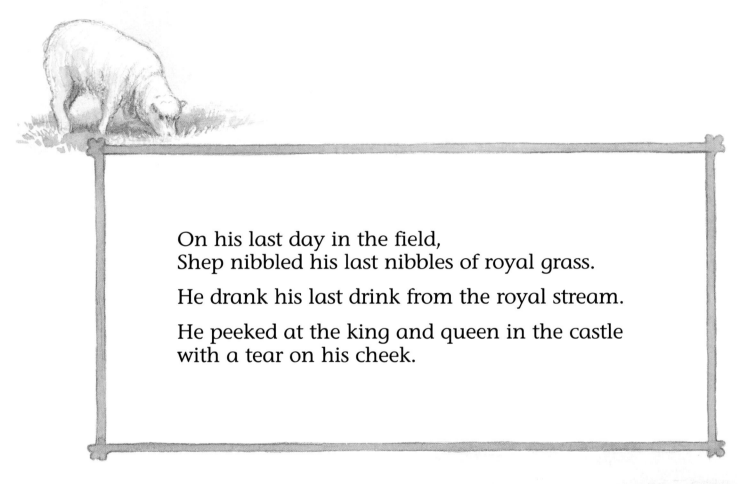

On his last day in the field,
Shep nibbled his last nibbles of royal grass.

He drank his last drink from the royal stream.

He peeked at the king and queen in the castle
with a tear on his cheek.

What Shep did not
understand was that
the king and queen
had a plan...

Their plan was
to make Shep's fleece
into the most beautiful
dress and jacket
in all of Caladeen.

21

Chapter 4

That night, as the queen and king slept, Shep crept from the royal field.
He peeked back at the rest of the sheep. He bleated a soft bleat.
Then he jumped and ran down the steep hill to the sea.

In the castle, the queen was up.

She ran to get the royal trackers.

"Get up, get up," the queen pleaded.

"I cannot hear Shep's bell. He must be lost!"

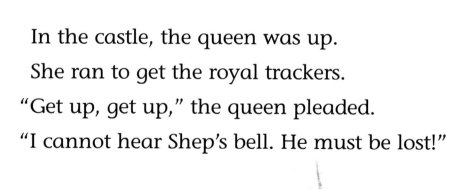

The royal trackers jumped on their steeds and galloped off into the night.

Half of them went east with the king, and half went west with the queen.

The hill was steeper than Shep had planned.
He slipped on mud and rocks.
Twigs stuck into his soft fleece.

Shep felt weak. Sad and in distress,
he hid next to a big stump and fell asleep.

As the sun crept up past the hill of Caladeen, Shep was not to be seen.

Filled with grief, the queen sat on a stump next to a big rock.

"Where could Shep be?" she asked.

And then there was a soft bleat…

The rock was not a rock, it was Shep!